GRANDPA'S GARDEN

In memory of my Grandpa, William Hubert Woodyard,
and to Kathryn and J. P. Montgomery,
for taking up where he left off. — *Shea Darian*

To three generations of very special women in my life,
my mother Lucille, my daughter Renee,
and my granddaughter Brianna. — *Karlyn Holman*

Published by DAWN Publications
14618 Tyler Foote Road
Nevada City, CA 95959
916 292-3482

Library of Congress Cataloging-in-Publication
(Prepared by Quality Books, Inc.)

Darian, Shea, 1959-
Grandpa's garden / Shea Darian ; illustrated by Karlyn Holman/
p. cm.
ISBN: 1-883220-42-4 (hardback)
ISBN: 1-883220-41-6 (paperback)

I. Holman, Karlyn, ill. II. Title.

PZ7.D375Gran 1996   [E]
QBI95-20655

Printed on recycled paper using soy based ink

Printed in Hong Kong

10 9 8 7 6 5 4 3 2 1
First Edition

Designed by LeeAnn Brook Design
Type style is Caslon 540

A Note from the Author

Gardens have been places of wonder to me for as long as I can remember. It all started with my grandfather, who welcomed me to such a patch of land—a garden which, for me, held as much wisdom and beauty as any place on earth. For in my Grandpa's garden I learned first-hand of the life and death, the growth and change of which a garden speaks.

For Grandpa and me, his garden was a place we shared our deepest feelings, thoughts, and wishes. It was a place I harvested the goodness of Grandpa's humor and wisdom about life, which has proven its usefulness over many years. I hope Grandpa's Garden and the gardening celebrations that follow will inspire you and those you care for to see gardens as places where love and wisdom can grow alongside the vegetables, fruits, and flowers.

On Saturdays I work in Grandpa's garden.

Here with the peas and turnips,

we talk about the mysteries of life:

why Ms. Fowler (who lives around the corner) always wears her sunbonnet off kilter,

how a pole bean finds its climbing pole,

and why my older brother never seems to see me anymore,

now that Alice Maken smiles at him when he says hello.

On Saturdays I work in Grandpa's garden.
Here with the strawberries and tomatoes,
I tell him things that no one knows but him and me:
that one day I want to be a great actor, or the world's fastest runner,
and that one day I want to make friends with the deaf girl down the street.

On Saturdays I work in Grandpa's garden.

Here with the radishes and lettuce,

and the garden fairy who's lived here since I can remember.

We pretend the fairy grants us each three wishes.

I wish to find a four-leaf clover, to learn to skate backwards,

and to have three more wishes.

He wishes for a jar of homemade preserves,
that his corn will grow healthy and tall,
and that when he gets to heaven, just once,
he can get a glimpse of
"our Maker's face,
full of love and shinin'
like the sun."

On Saturdays I work in Grandpa's garden.

The heat of the sun makes sweat beads under our straw hats.

I watch Grandpa's face, fix in my mind the color of his eyes,

the wrinkles that come when he laughs,

and the way he folds his bandanna after he wipes the sweat away.

Some days we do not speak.

Grandpa says words are like shiny new dimes—

you should ask yourself if they're better off spent or sittin' in your pocket.

So we dig and plant, hum and sway,

and keep our words for another day.

Grandpa is like an old work horse.

Grandma says he never knows when to stop.

But one day he stops before the sun is high in the sky.

He stops long before I am tired or sweaty.

Grandpa sits down hard on an old sawed-off tree stump.

He grabs his arm and scrunches his face.

I run down the gravel drive like the wind,
yellin' for Grandma to come quick.
Everything happens so fast, the ambulance comes,
and Grandpa goes off to the hospital.
Grandma says his heart isn't working right,
that he needs to rest for a time until his heart is strong again.

On Saturdays I work in Grandpa's garden,

here without the soft hum of Grandpa's voice,

the voice that feeds the plants as much as the earth and sun and rain.

There is much to do, and Grandma says while Grandpa has his rest

she is looking to me to keep the weeds from taking over,

and to harvest the food when it is ready.

Sometimes I cry when I think of how much I miss Grandpa,

but Grandma says that is just fine

because my tears will feed the garden too.

The weather has been hot and dry,

so I take some compost from the pile Grandpa calls the "earthworm's delight."

I spread it around each plant the way Grandpa taught me,

and water the plants with the garden hose.

As I spray the garden, it glistens and drinks down the water.

In the misty spray, I can almost see Grandpa here with me.

He moves about the garden with his bushel basket,

gathering radishes and peas, spinach and turnips.

In my mind, he pulls up a radish, shakes it a bit, and sets it in my open hand.

He winks and tells me, "A little dirt never hurt anybody."

I smile, and pop the radish in my mouth, like an adventure.

On Saturdays, I work in Grandpa's garden.
Turning compost with a shovel,
I remember Grandpa saying troubles are like garbage in the
compost heap—scraps of food, dead leaves, dry grass.
Mix it all up and after a time that old smelly stuff
turns into good, rich food for the plants.
"Troubles are the compost of life," Grandpa would say,
"if you have patience to see what they turn into,
you see what first appears to be a trouble
can also be a gift.
Over time, troubles have a way
of makin' us healthy and strong."

Grandma tells me Grandpa is getting stronger,
and that tomorrow we'll go to the hospital for a visit.
I smile as I pick the first ripe tomatoes of the summer
and in my mind I hear Grandpa say, "Looks like a mighty fine year for tomatoes."
"Yes, Grandpa," I tell him, "And look at your corn, silky tops showin' already."

The next day I do some weeding in the garden.
Then I wash up "in a snap," as Grandpa would say,
and drive to the hospital with Grandma.

In Grandpa's room, he takes my hand and kisses it.
"Well, I almost got my wish this time," he says, "to see that face in heaven. . .
but no sight is more welcome to these old eyes than this little face."
Grandpa's eyes are shining as I hand him flowers from the garden.
I tell him how straight and tall his corn has grown.
He smiles, and says in a few days he'll see it for himself.

On Saturdays I work in Grandpa's garden,

here with Grandpa standing beside me again, healthy and tall like the corn.

We sing as we harvest the first ears of the season.

We pick cucumbers and gather beans.

Then we sit to rest, and I tell him how scared I was that he might not come back.

Grandpa says every day is a gift, and that I don't need to worry about him dying.

He says he is certain he will die one day, and then his wish will come true—

to get a glimpse of our Maker's face, full of love and shinin' like the sun.

On Saturdays I work in Grandpa's garden.

Here with the spiders and worms, we work long into the afternoon.

A pesky bee stings my ankle,

and I hop up and down, yelping like a puppy.

Grandpa picks some mint leaves from the patch by the house.

He chews up a few and lays them on my ankle,

tending to me carefully with his strong, wrinkled old hands.

On Saturdays I work on Grandpa's Garden.
The weeks pass by, and we harvest the plenty.
The smell of autumn is in the air,
and Grandpa is an old workhorse again.
We'll pull carrots and dig up rutabagas.

As we work, Grandpa tells me that life is like a garden,
sown with tiny seeds.
He says there is a season for growing, a season for harvesting,
and a season for letting the soil rest.
And I know it's true—for every autumn
Grandpa and I put the garden to sleep for the winter.
But it is not time for that yet.

Then after dinner, as we often do,
Grandpa and I sit by the garden to welcome the evening.
We listen to the crickets, and watch the sun spread out with its blanket of colors.
In the quiet, I figure Grandpa's wish has already come true.
For when I look into Grandpa's eyes, I see
a glimpse of that face already glowing there—
the one so full of love and shinin' like the sun.

Listening in the Garden

Mother Earth is our teacher, sharing with us important lessons about life.
To understand her, we learn to listen not only with our ears, but also with our eyes, hands and
hearts. There is no better place to hear these lessons than in the garden, which overflows with the
wonder and wisdom of our Mother, the Earth.

Listen to Mother Earth, here in the garden. Come quietly from time to time.

Through the quiet perhaps Mother Earth will speak of the soil as her skin—

in some places worn thin, in others, many inches deep.

Soil—made of tiny pieces of broken rock, dead plants and creatures

changed into earth by the powers of the wind, rain, ice and air.

Soil—which sometimes takes hundreds of years to become even

one inch of the covering for Mother Earth.

Soil—out of which grows the food for all the creatures of the world.

Mother Earth asks us to walk gently upon the soil, to remember always to

care for it as if our lives depend upon it—because all life does.

Listen to Mother Earth, here in the garden. Come quietly from time to time.

Through the quiet, perhaps Mother Earth will speak of the wonder of

seeds, such tiny flakes, little balls and oblong shapes no bigger than the tip of a finger.

Seeds—called the "keepers of secrets" for keeping their secrets all winter long.

Seeds—that seem dead as we hold them in our hands, yet they are

the tiny, humble homes of a bounteous harvest.

Seeds—which when planted will be coaxed by earth, rain, and sun

to grow into plants hundreds, thousands, even millions of times larger.

Listen to Mother Earth, here in the garden. Come quietly from time to time.

Through the quiet perhaps Mother Earth will speak of the tireless worms,

eaters of dirt and dying plants.

Worms—whose daily food weighs more than they do, and whose

bodies turn that food into rich soil to feed the growing garden.

Worms—who are like little plows, tunneling endlessly through the

earth to make room for air and water to feed the roots.

Worms—who work on through the winter, while most of us other gardeners rest.

Mother Earth loves these wet and crawling creatures, for whom we hold so

little affection. She reminds us that the worm is our brother.

Listen to Mother Earth, here in the garden.

Come quietly from time to time.

Come at sunrise when dewdrops greet the morning.

Come in sunshine, wind and rain.

Come to hear the crickets sing at dusk.

Come on a night lit up by the face of a full moon.

Come to the garden to honor the great and the small of life,

to love and be loved, to give and receive,

and always to grow and change.

Celebrating Life in the Garden

People throughout the ages and of many cultures have gathered in gardens to bless the seeds and the soil. In garden ceremonies people have called upon the gifts of the sun, rain, air, and earth, summoned the aid of divine beings, performed sacred dances, lifted up prayers in song, and celebrated great harvest festivals. The garden holds a compelling power over us, not only because it reminds us of our need for food to sustain our physical bodies, but also because it gives us dramatic evidence that in this life we are co-creators with unseen powers. In the garden, we begin to understand our deeper connections with the unseen, with the earth, and with one another.

The gardening celebrations which follow are meant to inspire your own creativity. When my spouse, Andrew, and I create celebrations for our family, we include appropriate songs, verses, or prayers, perhaps a folk tale or nature story, or a simple circle dance. With young children, it is helpful to keep verbal explanations brief. Simply guiding children through the celebration allows the experience to speak for itself.

Our Creative Kin: A Ground-Breaking Ceremony

After you have broken ground in the spring, gather to bless your garden. You may wish to celebrate what I call the "kindoms of creation" that together nurture the future harvest: the earth, the plants, the animals, and humanity. To celebrate the gifts of the earth, you might pass a bowl of rich soil, so each person can take a handful and spread it over the garden. To celebrate the gifts of the plants, you may have each person place some seedling markers into the garden plot, or do a bit of planting. To celebrate the animals, you could offer a box of earthworms to your garden. To celebrate human gifts you might pass a hoe or pitcher of water and allow each person to offer a symbolic gesture of tending to the garden's needs.

Sowing Our Visions: A Seed Blessing

Consider blessing your garden seeds before planting. Allow children to inspect the various types of seeds. Speak briefly of the wonder of these tiny seeds, which are planted into the soil and burst from their skins to sprout with new life. Speak of how these seeds are like the hopes we have for our lives—to learn to roller skate, make a new friend, or grow a healthy garden. Have each person plant some seeds to symbolize their vision for the future. Before each person waters their seeds, they can share their special hope. Consider writing these visions on the back of your garden markers.

The Gift of Garbage: Celebrating the Compost of Life

When you are experiencing a problem, use your compost pile as a positive symbol of change. Toss compost onto the pile (a bouquet of wilted flowers works well), and name your concerns about the trouble. Then speak briefly of the way the elements work together to change garbage into rich soil which helps the plants to grow. Affirm that troubles can also bring us unexpected gifts. Gather at the compost pile again in several weeks to consider what gifts have come out of your trouble. Perhaps someone has reached out to help you, or what seemed to be a problem was actually an opportunity to make a needed change. This ceremony is also useful in saying "good-bye" at such times as before a move, or after the death of a pet. Toss compost onto the pile and name the specific things that will be missed. Afterwards, turn the pile with a pitchfork or shovel and name your special memories, lessons, and gifts you have received from this place or pet. Allow everyone's thoughts and feelings to flow freely and honestly.

All Good Gifts: A Harvest Celebration

When you have gathered the last of your harvest (or perhaps the first fruits), consider celebrating an evening harvest ritual. Build a fire, tell stories, sing songs, dance together. Offer thanks to the earth, rain, air, and sun, as well as to the more invisible creative powers. Share memories of the changes and events experienced during the gardening season. Celebrate the harvest of your lives, as well as the harvest of the garden.

About the Author and Illustrator

Shea Darian grew up in Urbandale, Iowa. She received a B.A. in Speech Communications and Theater from Iowa State University, a Master of Divinity degree from Garrett-Evangelical Seminary, and trained in Waldorf school administration and community development at the Waldorf Institute of Sunbridge College. Shea is a writer, workshop leader, singer and songwriter. Her first book, *Seven Times the Sun: Guiding Your Child Through the Rhythms of the Day*, was published by LuraMedia in 1994. Shea lives in Brookfield, Wisconsin with her spouse, Andrew, and their daughters, Morgan and Willa.

Karlyn Holman's watercolors reflect a special exuberance for her native area of Lake Superior. Karlyn has an M.A. in art from the University of Wisconsin and has taught at the college level for twelve years. She is a full-time artist and owns Karlyn's Gallery. She teaches high-spirited watercolor workshops throughout the world. This is the third book that she has illustrated. Karlyn lives with her husband Gary in Washburn, Wisconsin.

Acknowledgments

I extend my heart-felt thanks to those who have helped to cultivate Grandpa's Garden: Lura Geiger, for the imaginative seed, Ana Cerro, for coaxing the story out of me, Maggie Jezreel, for her ideas and insights, Rebecca Danica, for the magic of her encouragement, Andrew, Morgan, and Willa Darian, who give me daily inspiration, my publisher, Bob Rinzler, for his expertise and his faith in this project, Glenn Hovemann, for his sensitive and insightful editing, Karlyn Holman, who has so lovingly brought these pages to life, and finally, my mother, Demetra Anne Woodyard, who has carried this story in her heart perhaps even longer than I. — *Shea Darian*

I would like to thank the following people who have made this illustrating adventure a reality: Brianna, my Mom and Keith Carlson for their joyful cooperation in being my models; Renee Holman for her constant encouragement and for finding Mr. Carlson and The Blue Vista Farm; Amy Kalmon for her help in photographing some of my reference materials; my many artist friends, especially Bonnie, Elisabeth, Jan, Mary, June, and Karen for sharing their references and their insightful comments; Shea Darian for her inspiring text and helpful suggestions regarding her visual conception for the book; Bob Rinzler for his faith in my abilities to illustrate the book; LeeAnn Brook for her creative talent in putting the book together. — *Karlyn Holman*

Americans at War

TIMELINE *of the*
WAR ON
TERROR

By Charlie Samuels

Gareth Stevens
Publishing

Please visit our website www.garethstevens.com. For a free color catalog of all our high-quality books, call toll free 1-800-542-2595 or fax 1-877-542-2596.

Library of Congress Cataloging-in-Publication Data
Samuels, Charlie, 1961-
Timeline of the war on terror / Charlie Samuels.
    p. cm. — (Americans at war: a Gareth Stevens timeline series)
Includes index.
ISBN 978-1-4339-5924-0 (pbk.)
ISBN 978-1-4339-5925-7 (6-pack)
ISBN 978-1-4339-5922-6 (library binding)
1. War on Terrorism, 2001-2009—Juvenile literature. 2. War on Terrorism, 2001-2009—Chronology—Juvenile literature. 3. Terrorism—United States—Prevention—Juvenile literature. 4. Terrorism—Prevention—Juvenile literature. I. Title.
HV6432.S256 2012
973.931—dc22

                                                                                    2011010327

Published in 2012 by
Gareth Stevens Publishing
111 East 14th Street, Suite 349
New York, NY 10003

© 2012 Brown Bear Books Ltd.

For Brown Bear Books Ltd:
Editorial Director: Lindsey Lowe
Managing Editor: Tim Cooke
Children's Publisher: Anne O'Daly
Art Director: Jeni Child
Designer: Karen Perry
Picture Manager: Sophie Mortimer
Production Director: Alastair Gourlay

Picture Credits:
Front Cover: US Department of Defense

Key: t = top, b = bottom
Corbis: Sean Adair/Reuters 6; Jefri Aries/Zuma Press 39; Badri Media/epa 19, Paco Campos/epa 24; Ed Darack/Science Faction 13, 17; Carlos Dias/epa 21t; epa 33; Ric Ergenbright 28; Akhtar Gulfam/epa 27; Antoine Gyori/AGP 23b; Abed al Hafiz 37, Noor Khamis/Reuters 21b; Peter Macdiarmid/epa 22; Brendan McDermid/Reuters 44; Nabil Mounzer/epa 34; John Stanmeyer/VII 38; Mark Peterson 8; Andy Rain/epa 25; Romeo Ranoco/Reuters 40t; Reuters 7, 15, 32, 41; Adam Reynolds 35; Syed Jan Sabawoon/epa 17b; Richard Sennott/Zuma Press 45b; Jayanta Shaw/Reuters 26; Michelle Shephard/Zuma Press 42; Ramin Talaie 45t; Times of India/Reuters 29t; Goran Tomasevic/Reuters 30; Wang Ye/XinHua/Xinhua Press 29b; Adi Weda/epa 9t; Max Whittaker 16; **Shutterstock:** Alan Freed 9b; Amanda Haddox 12; Paolo Omero 11; Lizette Potgieter 10; **U.S. Army:** 18, 19, 19b; **U.S. Department of Defense:** 14, 20, 23t, 40b, 43

All Artworks © Brown Bear Books Ltd.

Publisher's note to educators and parents: Our editors have carefully reviewed the websites that appear on p. 47 to ensure that they are suitable for students. Many websites change frequently, however, and we cannot guarantee that a site's future contents will continue to meet our high standards of quality and educational value. Be advised that students should be closely supervised whenever they access the Internet.

Manufactured in the United States of America
1 2 3 4 5 6 7 8 9 12 11 10

CPSIA compliance information: Batch #BRS11GS: For further information contact Gareth Stevens, New York, New York at 1-800-542-2595.

Contents

Introduction   4

September 11   6

The War on Terror Begins   10

Afghanistan   14

Africa   18

Europe   22

India and Pakistan   26

Iraq   30

The Middle East   34

Southeast Asia   38

The United States   42

Glossary   46

Further Reading   47

Index   48

Introduction

The terrorist attacks of September 11, 2001, on New York and Washington, DC, sparked a worldwide reaction against terrorism, led by the United States.

The attacks of 9/11 were carried out by al-Qaeda, a global organization motivated by a desire to establish Islamic regimes around the world. For fundamentalist Islamists, the West is an enemy both because of its colonial past and because they believe that values such as democracy and civil rights are contrary to the Koran, the holy book of Islam. The vast majority of the world's 1.5 billion Muslims disagree with such an interpretation of the Koran and completely reject violence.

The Course of the War

In 2002, US president George W. Bush launched what he called a "war on terror." Its initial target was al-Qaeda, whose leaders were in hiding in Afghanistan. A US-led coalition invaded and toppled the Islamist Taliban government. The conflict also spread to other countries. In particular, US leaders identified the Iraqi regime of Saddam Hussein as a potential source of terrorism. In 2003, they invaded and overthrew Saddam. However, coalition troops faced an insurgency by Islamist fighters. In Afghanistan, too, the Taliban continued to fight. A form of democratic government was established in both countries, but a decade after the start of the "war," it was not clear whether it was being won—or whether it could be won. Terrorists continued to mount attacks in Europe and elsewhere.

About This Book

This book contains two types of timelines. Along the bottom of the pages is a timeline that covers the whole period. It lists key events and developments, color coded to indicate their part in the war. Each chapter also has its own timeline, which runs vertically down the sides of the pages. This timeline gives more specific details about the particular subject of the chapter.

US soldiers detonate explosives in the desert in the Horn of Africa in 2004 during Operation Enduring Freedom. ⬇

September 11

Most Americans were unaware of the Islamist group known as al-Qaeda until a series of spectacular terrorist attacks on September 11, 2001.

Smoke billows from the North Tower of the World Trade Center as the second airliner strikes the South Tower. ⇒

Timeline
2000
January–December

January 3 Jordan Planned attacks on three targets are thwarted; al-Qaeda is blamed for the plot.

January   May

KEY:

Iraq

Afghanistan

International

January 3 United States Al-Qaeda is suspected of being behind a failed plot to bomb Los Angeles International Airport.

At 8:46 on the morning of 9/11, a hijacked airliner crashed into the North Tower of the World Trade Center in New York. Seventeen minutes later, another aircraft flew into the South Tower. The Twin Towers both later collapsed, as did another building in the complex. At 9:37 A.M., a third jet crashed into the Pentagon in Washington, DC. A fourth passenger airline crashed in a field in Pennsylvania at 10:03; it was later learned that passengers had fought with the hijackers, whose target was probably the White House or the Capitol building in Washington, DC.

In all, some 2,996 people died, including the 19 hijackers, all the people on the four aircraft, and more than 340 New York City firefighters who were trying to rescue people from the World Trade Center when the buildings collapsed. Citizens from more than 90 countries died in the attacks, which caused outrage throughout the world.

The Chief Suspects

Within only a few hours, the Federal Bureau of Investigation had identified the hijackers responsible for the

Timeline

8:46 A.M. September 11, 2001 American Airlines Flight 11 from Boston's Logan Airport, bound for Los Angeles, hits the North Tower of the World Trade Center in New York City.

9:03 A.M. United Airlines Flight 175 bound for Los Angeles hits the South Tower of the World Trade Center, New York City.

9:05 A.M. At Booker Elementary School, Sarasota, Florida, President Bush is told "America is under attack."

9:37 A.M. American Airlines Flight 77 from Washington to Los Angeles crashes into the west side of the Pentagon.

(continued page 8)

← Two of the terrorists pass through airport security on the morning of the attacks.

October 20 Yemen In an al-Qaeda attack, the US navy destroyer USS *Cole* is rammed by a small boat carrying explosives, killing 17 sailors and injuring 39.

September

December

September 28 Israel The Palestinians begin a new intifada, or uprising, against Israeli occupation.

December 5 Jordan A Jordanian is sentenced to death for planning millennium attacks on US and Israeli targets.

Timeline (continued)

9:57 A.M. Passengers revolt on hijacked United Airlines Flight 93 from Newark.

9:58 A.M. South Tower of the World Trade Center starts to collapse.

10:03 A.M. Flight 93 crashes into a field in Pennsylvania.

10:10 A.M. Part of the west side of the Pentagon collapses.

10:28 A.M. The North Tower of the World Trade Center collapses 1 hour, 41 minutes, and 45 seconds after the plane's impact.

10:43 A.M. Mayor Rudolph Giuliani orders the evacuation of Lower Manhattan.

8:30 P.M. President Bush addresses the nation from the White House.

11:30 P.M. President Bush notes in his journal that the Americans suspect Osama bin Laden of the attacks.

attacks. Their ringleader was Mohamed Atta, from Egypt; the others were also Arabs, including 15 from Saudi Arabia. They had spent some months in the United States before boarding the flights at Boston, Newark, and Washington, DC. Evidence linked the hijackers to an Islamist group known as al-Qaeda, led by the Saudi Osama bin Laden. Bin Laden financed the suicide plot, which was planned by another al-Qaeda leader, Khalid Sheikh Mohammed.

An Enemy of America

Al-Qaeda had been founded by Osama bin Laden in 1979 in Afghanistan, where Muslim fighters were resisting the Soviet invasion.

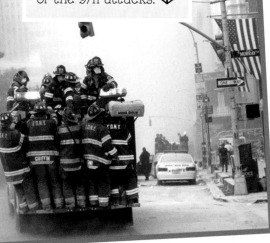

Firefighters in New York in the aftermath of the 9/11 attacks. ⇓

After the Soviets left Afghanistan in 1989, bin Laden turned his attention to the United States. In 1996, he announced that all US forces should leave Saudi Arabia, where they had been based since the Persian Gulf War against Iraq in 1990. In 1998, he issued further threats against the United States. That same year, al-Qaeda

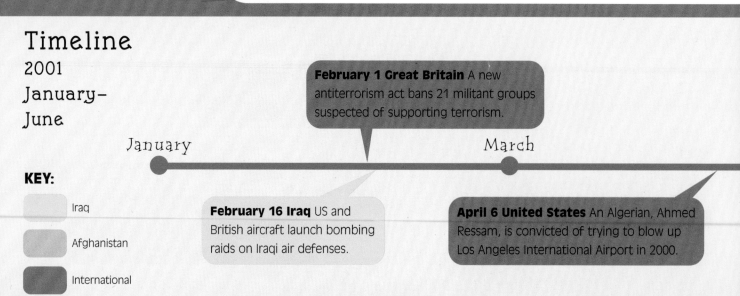

Timeline
2001
January–June

KEY:

- Iraq
- Afghanistan
- International

January

March

February 1 Great Britain A new antiterrorism act bans 21 militant groups suspected of supporting terrorism.

February 16 Iraq US and British aircraft launch bombing raids on Iraqi air defenses.

April 6 United States An Algerian, Ahmed Ressam, is convicted of trying to blow up Los Angeles International Airport in 2000.

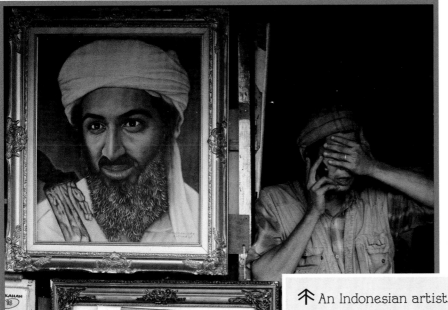

↑ An Indonesian artist displays his portrait of Osama bin Laden.

Flight 93

The only one of the four hijacked airplanes to miss its intended target was Flight 93. The passengers aboard learned about the other hijackings from calls to loved ones made on the airphones. The passengers decided to act to overpower the hijackers and take control of the flight deck. Their efforts crashed the plane into a field in Pennsylvania. All 44 passengers, including the four hijackers, were killed.

bombed the US Embassies in Kenya and Tanzania.

Bin Laden was believed to be sheltered by the radical Islamic Taliban government in Afghanistan. The United States gathered a broad alliance to help topple the Taliban and capture bin Laden. At the same time, the PATRIOT Act gave the US government greater powers to monitor suspected terrorists at home, despite many complaints that the act's provisions interfered with civil liberties.

← A monument marks the site where Flight 93 crashed.

May 26 Afghanistan The UN Security Council reports that the Taliban is selling heroin and opium to raise funds to train terrorists.

May

June

May 9 Afghanistan The Taliban close UN offices in retaliation for the imposition of UN sanctions.

June 15 India Security forces disrupt bombers sent by al-Qaeda to attack the US Embassy in New Delhi.

The War on Terror Begins

The first target of the US campaign was Osama bin Laden's al-Qaeda, which was sheltered by the Taliban government of Afghanistan.

Northern Alliance fighters ride into Kabul after the Taliban fled the Afghan capital. →

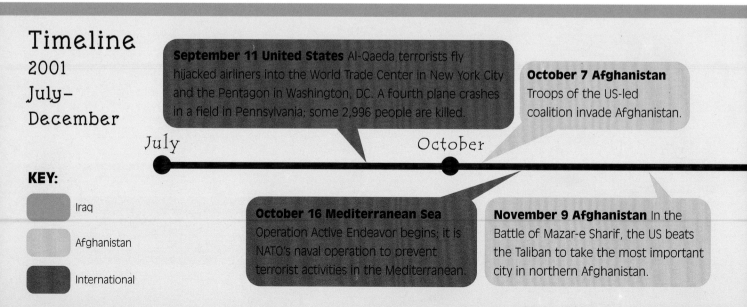

Timeline
2001
July–December

September 11 United States Al-Qaeda terrorists fly hijacked airliners into the World Trade Center in New York City and the Pentagon in Washington, DC. A fourth plane crashes in a field in Pennsylvania; some 2,996 people are killed.

October 7 Afghanistan Troops of the US-led coalition invade Afghanistan.

July   October

KEY:

Iraq

Afghanistan

International

October 16 Mediterranean Sea Operation Active Endeavor begins; it is NATO's naval operation to prevent terrorist activities in the Mediterranean.

November 9 Afghanistan In the Battle of Mazar-e Sharif, the US beats the Taliban to take the most important city in northern Afghanistan.

On September 20, 2001, George W. Bush told the US Congress that "our war on terror begins with al-Qaeda, but it does not end there. It will not end until every terrorist group of global reach has been found, stopped, and defeated." Later, in January 2002, Bush went on to identify an "axis of evil": countries that used or would potentially be prepared to use terrorism as part of state strategy—Iran, Iraq, and North Korea.

The Taliban

In the immediate aftermath of the attacks of 9/11, the United States' first target was Osama bin Laden and the Taliban government that harbored him in Afghanistan. The Taliban had come to power in 1996, following the withdrawal of Soviet troops from Afghanistan. These "students" promoted a strict form of Islam. .

Cleanup continues at "Ground Zero," the site of the World Trade Center. ⇊

Timeline

September 20, 2001 President George W. Bush uses the phrase "war on terror" in an address to Congress.

September 22, 2001 Saudi Arabia and the United Arab Emirates withdraw recognition of the Taliban as the government of Afghanistan; now only Pakistan acknowledges the government.

October 7, 2001 US and British jets begin bombing targets in Afghanistan.

November 9, 2001 Northern Alliance forces claim the city of Mazar-e Sharif.

November 13, 2001 Northern Alliance forces enter the Afghan capital, Kabul, after it is abandoned by the Taliban.

November 25, 2001 US forces establish their first base in Afghanistan, Camp Rhino.

(continued page 12)

November 12–25 Afghanistan Kunduz falls to alliance troops. It is the last Taliban garrison in the north of Afghanistan.

December 13 India Islamist gunmen attack Parliament in New Delhi; India blames the attack on Pakistan-based groups.

December 22 Afghanistan Hamid Karzai becomes head of a power-sharing government.

December

December 7 Afghanistan Coalition forces conquer the last Taliban stronghold, Kandahar.

December 22 United States Richard Reid, a British Islamic fundamentalist, tries but fails to detonate explosives hidden in his shoe on a transatlantic flight.

Timeline (continued)

January 29, 2002 President George W. Bush identifies an "axis of evil"—Iran, Iraq, and North Korea—as potential sponsors of terrorism and targets for US operations.

January 16, 2002 The United Nations Security Council starts an arms embargo on Afghanistan and freezes assets belonging to Osama bin Laden.

January 15, 2002 Some 1,200 US special forces arrive in the Philippines as part of Operation Enduring Freedom.

March 11, 2002 George W. Bush offers US assistance to any government to combat terrorism.

June 7, 2002 George W. Bush reveals plans for increased homeland security.

October 7, 2002 NATO forces arrive to advance Operation Enduring Freedom in the Horn of Africa.

They banned music and hobbies such as kite flying, prevented women from working or men from shaving, and blew up huge Buddhist statues that were recognized as a World Heritage Site by the United Nations. The Taliban had offered Osama bin Laden a safe haven after other Muslim countries had expelled him for his increasingly radical speeches and threats. Bin Laden's aim of creating fundamentalist Islamic states threatened moderate Muslim governments as much as it did Western governments.

Into Afghanistan

After the 9/11 attacks, the North Atlantic Treaty Organization (NATO) announced that it recognized the attack on the United States as an attack on all its members. There was a similar response from other parts of the world. The United States put together a coalition that was supported by dozens of nations, either in terms of military forces, supplies, bases, or in

George W. Bush declared a "war on terror" in January 2002. »

Timeline
2002 January–June

January 29 United States In his State of the Union address, George Bush identifies an "axis of evil" of Iran, Iraq, and North Korea.

February 1 Pakistan Islamic militants behead kidnapped US journalist Daniel Pearl.

January

March

KEY:

- Iraq
- Afghanistan
- International

January 1 Afghanistan The first foreign peacekeepers arrive in Afghanistan.

January 15 Philippines Operation Enduring Freedom begins in the Philippines.

April 11 Tunisia An al-Qaeda suicide bomber drives a gas tanker into a synagogue, killing 21 people.

permission for use of air bases. On Sunday, October 7, 2001, US and British aircraft started bombing Taliban targets.

The coalition campaign was aided by the Northern Alliance, a group of Afghan warlords in the north of the country that resented Taliban rule. The initial phase of the ground war was completed by November 26. Many of the Taliban fled to Pakistan. However, in the Battle of Tora Bora, US forces apparently missed a chance to capture Osama bin Laden.

个 A young Afghan watches as US soldiers search for al-Qaeda suspects in his home.

A Wider Operation

As Operation Enduring Freedom began in Afghanistan, other parts of the operation began in countries that also feared Islamic extremism. They included operations in the Philippines, the Horn of Africa, the Sahara region, and later in the Caribbean and Kyrgyzstan.

Al-Qaeda

The chief target of Operation Enduring Freedom, al-Qaeda, was blamed for terror attacks around the world. It had been created in the late 1980s by the Saudi Osama bin Laden to support Muslims fighting the Soviet occupation of Afghanistan. Bin Laden's vast wealth allowed him to fund the organization with up to $30 million a year. Al-Qaeda, which means "the base" in Arabic, now encourages terrorist attacks aimed at creating strict Muslim states around the world.

May 9 Russia A bomb explosion at Victory Day celebrations in Dagestan kills 42 people.

June 13 Afghanistan The Loya Jirga tribal assembly chooses Hamid Karzai as the president.

May

June 14 Pakistan A car bomb near the US Embassy in Karachi kills 12 people.

Afghanistan

When the Americans led the coalition invasion of Afghanistan in 2001, little did US leaders know that the war would still be continuing 10 years later.

French soldiers of NATO's International Security Assistance Force patrol in Afghanistan. »

Timeline
2002
July–December

KEY:

Iraq

Afghanistan

International

July

October

October 12 Indonesia Bombs in the tourist resort of Bali kill 202 people, many of whom are Westerners and Australians.

September 12 United States President George W. Bush warns the United Nations of the growing threat from Iraq.

October 23–26 Russia Chechen separatists seize hostages in a theater in Moscow; an operation to release them leaves 120 hostages and 40 terrorists dead.

After al-Qaeda's September 11, 2001, attacks, the United States launched a war in Afghanistan to destroy the terrorist bases there and overthrow the Taliban, the country's fundamentalist Muslim rulers who harbored bin Laden. The campaign went well as the Taliban was removed from power and a pro-Western government was installed in the capital, Kabul.

To escape the US-led war in Afghanistan, al-Qaeda's leadership sought refuge across the border in Pakistan's tribal areas. Bin Laden, along with other members of the organization, went into hiding in Pakistan, where he was located and killed by U.S. special forces in 2011.

NATO in Afghanistan

As part of the war on terror, the United States was helped in Afghanistan by other members of the North Atlantic Treaty Organization (NATO). Since September 11, 2001, the allies have sought to create a "new" NATO, able to go beyond Europe to combat new threats, such

↑ Triumphant Northern Alliance troops enter Kabul on November 13, 2001.

Timeline

February 15, 1989 The Soviets withdraw from Afghanistan.

September 27, 1996 The Taliban seize Kabul.

September 11, 2001 Al-Qaeda terrorist attacks occur in the United States.

October 7, 2001 Operation Enduring Freedom is launched by the United States to destroy al-Qaeda safe havens, including those in Afghanistan.

November 13, 2001 Kabul falls to Northern Alliance.

December 3–17, 2001 Al-Qaeda members are forced out of the Tora Bora cave complex and escape to Pakistan.

December 22, 2001 Hamid Karzai is sworn in as head of an interim government.

(continued page 16)

November 28 Kenya A bomb attack on a hotel leaves 15 people dead.

December 27 Russia A bus bomb is used to blow up the Chechen parliament in Grozny, killing 83 people.

December

November 18 Iraq United Nations weapons inspectors arrive in Iraq to search for evidence of weapons of mass destruction.

Timeline (continued)

August 11, 2003 NATO takes over responsibility for security in Kabul, its first such duty outside Europe.

September 2005 Parliamentary elections held in Afghanistan for the first time in 30 years.

May–June 2006 Many Taliban killed in Operation Mountain Thrust in the south.

March 2007 Operation Achilles is another large thrust against the Taliban in the south.

September 2008 President Bush sends an extra 4,500 US troops to Afghanistan.

July 2009 US and Afghan forces begin a major operation in Helmand province.

July 2010 President Karzai formulates plan for Afghan forces to take charge of security by 2014.

as terrorism and the proliferation of weapons of mass destruction. Afghanistan is NATO's first "out of area" mission beyond Europe. The purpose of the mission is the stabilization and reconstruction of Afghanistan.

The NATO-led International Security Assistance Force (ISAF) faced many obstacles: shoring up a weak government in Kabul; using military capabilities in a distant country with rugged terrain; and also rebuilding a country devastated by war and troubled by a resilient narcotics trade. Although the allies agree on ISAF's mission goals, they differ on how to accomplish them. Until recently, only the United States wanted to engage directly in the destruction of poppy fields and drug facilities in attempts to destroy the illegal drug trade.

A US patrol explores the remote mountains of Kandahar province in 2009.

Rebuilding Afghanistan

The PRTs or Provincial Reconstruction Teams, made up of military and civilian officials, are charged with extending the reach of the Afghan government by improving governance and

Timeline
2003
January–June

January

March

KEY:

Iraq

Afghanistan

International

January 5 Israel Two Islamist bombers kill 23 people in coordinated attacks in Tel Aviv.

March 4 Philippines A bomb blast at Davao leaves 21 dead.

rebuilding the economy. There are differences in how individual NATO governments operate their PRTs. Increasing turmoil in Pakistan complicates efforts to prevent the Taliban from infiltrating Afghanistan.

Talking to the Taliban?

By 2008, it appeared that NATO's military effort in Afghanistan was failing. Violence in and around Kabul reached record highs, corruption was rampant, and pessimism rose. A US report said Afghanistan was in a "downward spiral," fueled by drug money and weak central government. It appeared that the only solution to the war in Afghanistan was a settlement with the Taliban, but talking to their enemy was something the Americans did not relish.

The US attack on Tora Bora failed to trap the al-Qaeda leaders. ➡

THE LOCATION OF THE TORA BORA CAVE COMPLEX

AFGHANISTAN

Kabul River

Jalalabad   Lalpur

Garikhil   Mileva

TORA BORA

PAKTIA PROVINCE

Gardez

Khost

KHOST PROVINCE

PAKITKA PROVINCE

PAKISTAN

⬅ An Afghan fighter keeps a lookout.

Battle of Tora Bora

Tora Bora is an ancient and vast cave complex near the Khyber Pass. Believing Osama bin Laden and his followers were hiding in the caves, Afghan forces attacked Tora Bora with the US Air Force providing air support in early December 2001.

On December 12, Afghan commanders opened negotiations with members of al-Qaeda. These talks led to many of them, including Osama bin Laden, being allowed to escape west into Pakistan.

March 17 Iraq President George Bush gives Saddam Hussein 48 hours to leave Iraq or face war.

May

March 20 Iraq A US-led military invasion topples the government of Saddam Hussein, who goes into hiding.

May 12 Saudi Arabia Al-Qaeda is blamed for suicide bomb attacks on compounds for US workers in Riyadh that kill 26 people.

Africa

The continuing rise of homegrown terrorism across Africa is a cause of grave concern to the United States as the reach of al-Qaeda appears to grow stronger.

A US soldier befriends a group of curious children in Djibouti in the Horn of Africa in March 2004. →

Timeline

2003
July–December

July

August

August 11 Afghanistan NATO takes control of security in the capital, Kabul.

August 25 India Two separate bombs in Mumbai kill a total of 50 people.

KEY:

Iraq

Afghanistan

International

July 13 Iraq A US-appointed governing council meets for the first time.

August 19 Iraq A suicide bombing wrecks the United Nations headquarters in Baghdad, killing the senior UN representative in the country.

↑ Soldiers wait to defend the Somali capital against Islamists in 2010.

At the start of the 21st century, the US military embarked on a long-term push into Africa to stop what it considered to be growing inroads by al-Qaeda and other terrorist networks in poor, lawless, and largely Muslim expanses of Algeria, Chad, Mali, Mauritania, Niger, Senegal, Nigeria, Morocco, and Tunisia.

The Pentagon planned to train thousands of African troops to fight together in desert and border operations.

Timeline

October 12, 2000 The USS *Cole* is attacked by a suicide bomber in the Yemeni port of Aden; 17 US sailors are killed.

November 28, 2002 In the coastal town of Mombasa, Kenya, the Army of Palestine, a previously unknown Lebanese group, bombs Israeli-owned targets; the United States condemns the attacks and vows to continue its "war on terror."

July 23, 2005 Following suicide bombings by a group claiming ties to al-Qaeda, which kill at least 88 people at the Egyptian resort of Sharm el-Sheik, the United States denounces continuing terror attacks.

April 23, 2006 Osama bin Laden criticizes a peace agreement in Sudan that had been made between the military-Islamist government and the Sudan People's Liberation Movement (SPLM) in January 2005.

(continued page 20)

November 8 Saudi Arabia
An expatriate living compound in al-Muhaya is attacked by a car bomb that kills 17 people.

December 14 Iraq Saddam Hussein is captured hiding in a hole in the ground near Tikrit.

November

December

December 5 Russia Suicide bombers attack a train in southern Russia, killing 46 people.

Timeline (continued)

June 11, 2007 President George W. Bush has given $1 billion in military and other aid to Kenya; a car bomb explodes near the US Embassy in Nairobi, the capital.

July 10, 2010 A bomb kills 74 people watching the World Cup finals in a bar in the Ugandan capital, Kampala; an Islamist Somali group claiming ties to al-Qaeda claims to have carried out the attack.

January 1, 2011 Islamic extremists bomb a Coptic church in Alexandria, Egypt, killing 23 Christian worshipers.

A US C-130 Hercules transport aircraft takes off from a Sudanese airfield. →

Terrorism in the Horn of Africa

The thrust into Africa was considered vital to head off infiltration by international terrorist groups. Small groups of Islamic radicals were moving into Africa from the conflict in Iraq, where Africans made up about a quarter of the foreign fighters.

Somalia

Somalia has given the most cause for concern. US strategy toward Somalia was three-fold: to eliminate the terrorist threat, to promote political stability, and to address the humanitarian crisis. Somalia proved far more complex than either the United States or its Ethiopian allies admitted, however. Since 1991, there has been no stable government. The Islamic Courts Union, which was the effective Somali government, was not recognized internationally but had popular support within Somalia, where it controlled most of the country.

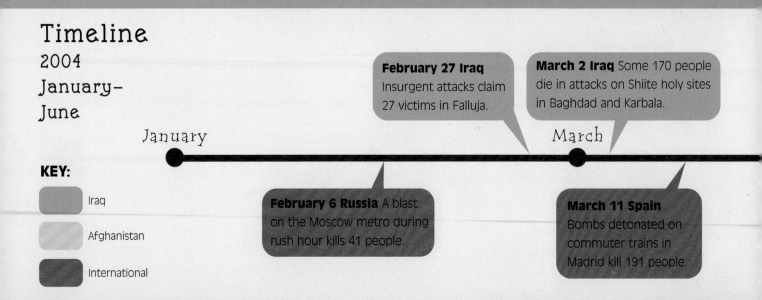

Timeline
2004
January–
June

January

KEY:

Iraq

Afghanistan

International

February 27 Iraq Insurgent attacks claim 27 victims in Falluja.

March 2 Iraq Some 170 people die in attacks on Shiite holy sites in Baghdad and Karbala.

March

February 6 Russia A blast on the Moscow metro during rush hour kills 41 people.

March 11 Spain Bombs detonated on commuter trains in Madrid kill 191 people.

Ongoing Violence

Ethiopia had secretly stationed troops in Somalia and, with US backing, invaded its neighbor in 2007.

Ethiopian troops quit Somalia in January 2009, shortly before a moderate Islamist Somali government was elected. The government was weak, however, and soon collapsed. In May 2009, Islamists again attacked the capital. The radical group al-Shabab proclaimed its allegiance to al-Qaeda and carried out a series of terrorist attacks.

UN Secretary-General Ban Ki-moon called for international support to bring stability to Somalia. However, Somali unrest spread to other parts of East Africa. In July 2010, al-Shabab bombed the Ugandan capital, Kampala, killing 74 people watching the World Cup final on TV. Religious and ethnic divisions continued to divide Sudan. Meanwhile, al-Qaeda still operated in the region, supported by al-Shabab.

Portuguese marines detain suspects in the Gulf of Aden.

Sudan

Sudan became the site of an ideological struggle between the United States and al-Qaeda. Sudan supported the "war on terror" but suffered from the expansion of al-Qaeda's presence in the country. By 2008, it was ranked as the third-most unstable country in the world. In a referendum in January 2011, people in southern Sudan—who are not Muslim—voted to split from the North.

← A Kenyan Muslim protests the deportation of a preacher suspected of terrorism.

April–May Iraq The Mehdi Army, Shia militia loyal to Mullah Moqtada al-Sadr, take on coalition forces in Iraq.

May 9 Russia The president of Chechnya is killed by a bomb at a stadium where he is attending a public event.

May

April 3 Spain The Madrid railroad bombers blow themselves up when they are cornered by police in Madrid.

June 28 Iraq US forces hand sovereignty in Iraq to the interim Iraqi government.

Europe

In the first decade of this century, bombs across Europe brought the realities of the Islamist war home to Europeans. Many of the terrorists were homegrown.

A suicide bomb tore ⇒ the roof off this London bus in the terrorist attacks of July 7, 2005.

Timeline
2004
July– December

August 5–27 Iraq Intense fighting continues in Najaf between US forces and the Shia militia of Moqtada al-Sadr.

September 1 Russia Separatist terrorists seize a school at Beslan, in North Ossetia, taking 1,100 people hostage; in an operation to free them three days later, 334 hostages die, including 186 children.

July

September

September 16 Afghanistan Taliban fire a rocket at a helicopter carrying President Hamid Karzai.

KEY:

Iraq

Afghanistan

International

↟ A US soldier hands out counterterrorism leaflets in Bosnia.

I n Europe, the terrorist threat came from numerous sources. In Spain, Basque nationalists continued an armed campaign against the government. In Northern Ireland, the Continuity IRA attacked Protestant targets. In both cases, however, the peak of violence had passed.

Elsewhere, nationalism combined with Islamism in struggles in the Caucasus region of southern Russia,

← A shrine to the children who died in the Beslan school siege.

Timeline

October 23, 2002 Armed Chechen attackers seize a crowded Moscow theater; in a later rescue attempt, at least 120 hostages die.

February 6, 2004 Suicide bombers on the Moscow metro kill at least 40 people.

March 11, 2004 Al-Queda supporters blow up commuter trains in Madrid, Spain, killing 191 people.

September 1, 2004 Armed Chechen separatists attack a school in Beslan, South Russia; in an attempted rescue, 334 hostages die, including 186 of the children.

(continued page 24)

October 7 Pakistan A car bomb kills 38 people at a Sunni religious rally.

December 19 Iraq A car bomb attack on a funeral procession in Najaf kills around 50 people.

October

December

November 7 Iraq US and Iraqi troops launch Operation Phantom Fury, a major campaign against insurgents in Fallujah.

Timeline (continued)

July 7, 2005 Suicide bombers target London with bombs on three subway trains and one bus; 52 people die.

August 10, 2006 A plot to blow up US-bound aircraft midflight is foiled in London.

June 27, 2007 A car rams into a terminal at Scotland's Glasgow Airport in a failed suicide bombing.

March 29, 2010 Female suicide bombers attack the Moscow metro, killing 40.

December 11, 2010 Two bombs in Stockholm, Sweden, kill the bomber.

January 24, 2011 A suicide bomber attacks Moscow's Domodedovo Airport, killing at least 35.

Badly destroyed rail carriages following the Madrid bombings. →

where separatists from republics such as Chechnya fought against Russian control. In 2002, Chechen terrorists seized a theater audience as hostages in the Russian capital, Moscow. In the police operation that followed, hundreds of hostages died. There were also numerous suicide bombings on the Moscow metro.

The most notorious Chechen attack came in 2004, when terrorists took hundreds of children and parents hostage in a school in Beslan, North Ossetia. Again, the police operation went wrong: some 334 hostages died. More than half of them were young children.

Western Europe

In western Europe, the Islamist threat was both internal and external. Muslim terrorists from North Africa were active in southern Europe, but many European countries produced homegrown terrorists. Young Muslims turned against the countries where they were raised. Often such individuals were motivated by resentment of Western

Timeline
2005
January–June

January

January 30 Iraq Millions of Iraqis vote in elections for a national assembly.

February 28 Iraq In Hilla, Baghdad, a car bomb leaves 114 people dead.

March

February 14 Lebanon A car bomb kills the former prime minister of Lebanon and some 20 other people.

KEY:

Iraq

Afghanistan

International

↑ Supporters of Jean Charles de Menezes call for an inquiry into his shooting by UK police.

support for Israel and interference in the Muslim world. North Africans blew up commuter trains in Madrid, Spain, in 2004 in retaliation for Spain's support for the invasion of Iraq. In 2005, British Muslims attacked subway trains and buses in London.

Successful Intelligence

Within Europe, the war on terror was largely an intelligence operation. Security forces disrupted a number of more or less serious plots before they were realized. There were also some attacks that failed due to the lack of skill of the terrorists.

Jean Charles de Menezes

On July 22, 2005, de Menezes, a Brazilian man living in London, was identified by antiterrorist police as a fugitive involved in failed bomb attacks in the city the previous day. The police followed him to a subway station, where they shot him dead. He was later found to be an innocent victim of mistaken identity. The British police were fined for the killing. The shoot-to-kill policy that had been adopted to deal with suicide bombers was abandoned.

May Iraq Some 672 civilians die in bomb attacks during May, representing a huge surge in the number of attacks.

May

April Egypt A number of attacks in April target tourist coaches and markets frequented by tourists.

India and Pakistan

Religious tensions that have marked the relationship between India and Pakistan since Partition in 1947 have worsened in the last decade.

Mumbai's famous Taj Mahal Palace hotel on fire during the terrorist attacks of 2008. →→

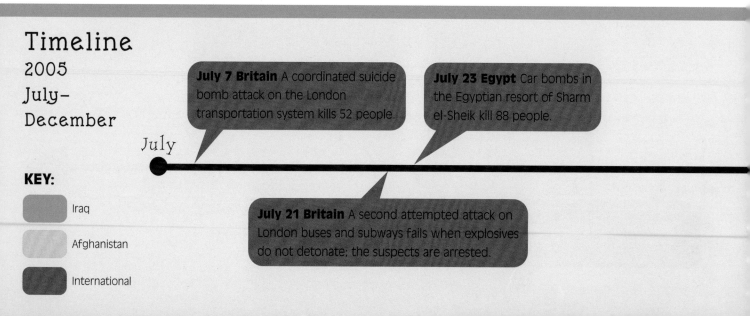

Timeline
2005
July–
December

July

KEY:

Iraq

Afghanistan

International

July 7 Britain A coordinated suicide bomb attack on the London transportation system kills 52 people.

July 23 Egypt Car bombs in the Egyptian resort of Sharm el-Sheik kill 88 people.

July 21 Britain A second attempted attack on London buses and subways fails when explosives do not detonate; the suspects are arrested.

↑ Pakistani police guard suspected members of the Taliban near the border with Afghanistan.

Timeline

August 25, 2003 In Mumbai, India, two car bombs near the Gateway of India and Zaveri bazaar kill 54 people.

October 7, 2004 In Multan, Pakistan, a car bomb kills 38 at a Sunni religious rally.

October 29, 2005 Three explosions in New Delhi, India, kill 60 and injure more than 200.

March 7, 2006 A bomb in the Hindu holy city of Varanasi, India, kills 28.

April 11, 2006 A suicide bomber kills 57 Sunni Muslims in Karachi, Pakistan.

July 11, 2006 Seven coordinated bombs explode in Mumbai, India, killing 209.

August 25, 2007 Twin bombs detonated in Hyderabad, India, kill 44 people.

(continued page 28)

Following the 9/11 attacks and the US-led invasion of Afghanistan that followed, leaders of al-Qaeda and the Afghan Taliban, along with several other terrorist groups, fled across the border into Pakistan. Al-Qaeda's leader, Osama bin Laden, eventually settled in the Pakistani city of Abbottabad. At the start of May 2011, he was shot dead there when U.S. special forces raided his secret compound.

The Taliban dominated the northwestern Swat Valley, from which it was suspected of launching various terrorist attacks on targets in major Pakistani cities. The Taliban vowed to increase its attacks after the

October 24 Iraq Car bombs outside the Green Zone in Baghdad kill 20 people.

September

September 18 Afghanistan Parliamentary elections are held in Afghanistan.

Timeline (continued)

October 18, 2007 Former Pakistani prime minister, Benazir Bhutto, survives a suicide bomb attack that kills 136 followers.

December 27, 2007 Benazir Bhutto is assassinated in Rawalpindi, Pakistan.

July 7, 2008 Pakistan is blamed for a suicide attack on the Indian Embassy in Kabul that kills 50.

September 20, 2008 A car bomb at the Marriott Hotel, Islamabad, Pakistan, kills 60 and injures 250.

November 26–29, 2008 More than 10 coordinated shooting and bomb attacks across Mumbai, India, kill at least 172.

December 2008 Press reports claim that Islamic militants now control more than 75 percent of Pakistan's Swat Valley.

May 1, 2011 Osama bin Laden is killed in a US special forces raid in Abbottabad, Pakistan.

The Swat Valley is → a base for the Taliban in Pakistan.

August 2009 killing by a US drone (unmanned bomber) of its then leader, Baitullah Mehsud. Meanwhile, the lawless northwest tribal region, which acts as a sanctuary for militants, threatened to become further destabilized in August 2010 by the worst floods to occur in Pakistan for 80 years, which affected some 20 million people throughout the north of the country.

The Mumbai Attacks

In November 2008, terrorists with bombs and guns attacked a range of targets in India's financial capital, Mumbai. The Indian government blamed Pakistan-based militants, further increasing tension between India and Pakistan. Yet cooperation between the two

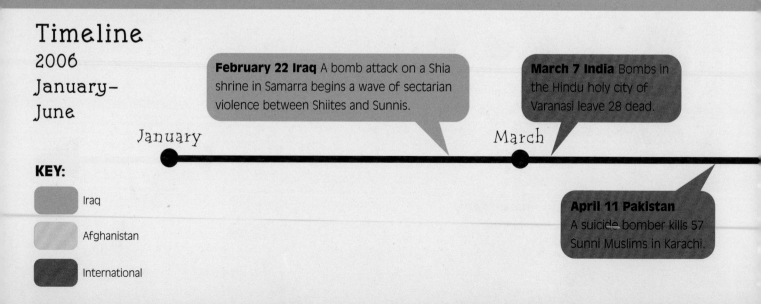

Timeline
2006 January– June

January

February 22 Iraq A bomb attack on a Shia shrine in Samarra begins a wave of sectarian violence between Shiites and Sunnis.

March 7 India Bombs in the Hindu holy city of Varanasi leave 28 dead.

March

April 11 Pakistan A suicide bomber kills 57 Sunni Muslims in Karachi.

KEY:

Iraq

Afghanistan

International

countries is vital to the "war on terror." To this end, in September 2008, the US government formed a "Friends for Pakistan" group to help Pakistan with development and stability. The group includes China and Saudi Arabia, which both have a considerable influence over Pakistan's political and military elite.

↑ Ajmal Kasab was the only terrorist to be caught alive after the Mumbai attacks.

The ISI Problem

The Mumbai attacks renewed suspicions that the Pakistani government, particularly its intelligence agency, the Inter-Services Intelligence (ISI), might not wholly support Washington's fight against terrorism. In May 2011, the United States gave Pakistan no warning of the special forces raid on Osama bin Laden's compound during which the terrorist was shot dead. Pakistan was forced to admit that its intelligence services had been unaware of bin Laden's presence in the country. Some voices in the US administration expressed doubts that the claim could be true.

The Assassination of Benazir Bhutto

Benazir Bhutto (1953–2007) was the first woman to lead an Islamic state. She served two terms as Pakistan's prime minister (1988–1990 and 1993–1996). In 2007, she returned from self-imposed exile to campaign in elections. Almost instantly, she was targeted by Islamic terrorists. She was killed at a rally in Rawalpindi on December 27, 2007. An attacker shot her before blowing himself up.

⇐ An Indian commando runs for cover during the Mumbai attacks.

June 2–3 Canada Police in Canada arrest 17 alleged Islamic terrorists.

May

June

May–June Afghanistan US and NATO forces launch Operation Mountain Thrust against the Taliban; there are scores of dead on both sides.

June 7 Iraq The al-Qaeda leader in Iraq, Abu Musab al-Zarqawi, is killed in an American airstrike.

Iraq

The invasion of Iraq and removal of its ruler, Saddam Hussein, was not an original aim of the "war on terror" but became crucial to its success.

A US soldier watches as a statue of Saddam Hussein is pulled down in central Baghdad in April 2003. ⟶

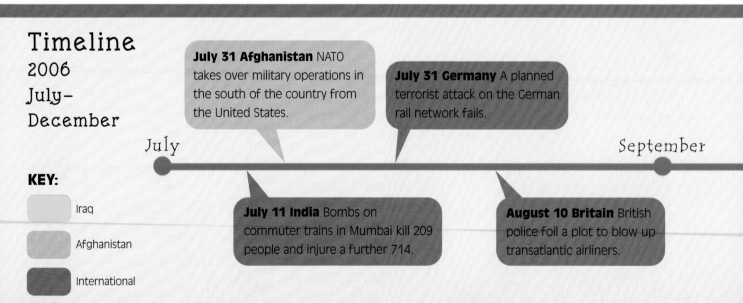

Timeline
2006
July–December

KEY:

Iraq

Afghanistan

International

July

September

July 31 Afghanistan NATO takes over military operations in the south of the country from the United States.

July 31 Germany A planned terrorist attack on the German rail network fails.

July 11 India Bombs on commuter trains in Mumbai kill 209 people and injure a further 714.

August 10 Britain British police foil a plot to blow up transatlantic airliners.

Operation Iraqi Freedom (OIF)—the US-led coalition's military operation in Iraq—began on March 20, 2003. The immediate goal, as argued by the Bush administration as a justification for going to war, was to remove Saddam Hussein's regime. The United States and its allies claimed it was necessary to destroy Saddam's ability to build or use weapons of mass destruction or to make them available to terrorists.

Rebuilding Iraq

After initial combat operations quickly drove Saddam from power, the focus of OIF shifted to the more open-ended mission of helping an emerging new Iraqi leadership. Over time, serious challenges to the Iraqi leadership grew from both homegrown insurgents and foreign fighters. The February 2006 bombing of the

THE 2003 INVASION OF IRAQ

KURDISH REGION
NO-FLY ZONE
U.S. ATTACK

(continued page 32)

Timeline

March 20, 2003 A US-led coalition begins the military invasion of Iraq.

December 14, 2003 Saddam Hussein is captured.

November 7–December 23, 2004 The Battle for Fallujah ends in a victory for US forces.

December 15, 2005 Iraqis vote for the first full-term government since the invasion.

February 22, 2006 A bomb attack on a mosque in Samarra begins an upsurge in violence between Shiites and Sunnis.

The invasion of Iraq was a short operation: It lasted less than a month.

November 23 Iraq Car bombs and mortar attacks kill around 215 people in Sadr City, Baghdad.

December 30 Iraq Saddam Hussein is hanged.

November

October 5 Afghanistan NATO takes control of military operations throughout the country.

December 6 United States Nation-of-Islam convert Derrick Shareef is arrested during his plans to launch an attack on an Illinois shopping mall.

Timeline (continued)

December 30, 2006 Saddam Hussein is executed.

January 10, 2007 President Bush announces troop surge.

March 25–31, 2008 Iraqi forces reclaim much of Basra from militia control.

January 1, 2009 Iraq takes control of security in Baghdad's Green Zone.

February 27, 2009 President Obama announces withdrawal of US troops by next year.

October 25, 2009 Two car bombs kill at least 155 people, the deadliest attacks since April 2007.

August 19, 2010 The last US combat troops leave Iraq.

A US military policeman arrests a former Iraqi soldier. ⟫

Golden Mosque in Samarra began a rise in religious violence, largely between Shia and Sunni Muslims. The character of the war changed from major battles to a counterinsurgency (COIN) and reconstruction effort.

Change of Direction

In January 2007, in an attempt to reverse the escalation of violence, President George W. Bush announced a fresh strategic approach to Iraq, called the "New Way Forward." The strategy included a "surge" of additional US forces being sent to the country. The surge put into effect COIN approaches on the ground that were designed to promote population security, such as troops living among the local population at small outposts.

Over the course of the surge, security conditions on the ground improved significantly. In August 2008, the outgoing commanding general of Multinational Force–Iraq, US general David Petraeus, agreed that the surge had made "significant progress." However, he argued that progress toward peace and stablity in Iraq was "still not self-sustaining."

Timeline
2007
January–June

January 10 Iraq President George W. Bush announces a new strategy involving a "surge" of thousands more US troops in Iraq.

March 27 Iraq Shiite pilgrims are targeted by truck bombs at Tel Afar; 152 pilgrims die.

January

March

KEY:

Iraq

Afghanistan

International

March 16 Afghanistan NATO forces launch Operation Achilles against the Taliban in the south of the country.

Murals in Iran illustrate scenes of US mistreatment of prisoners in Abu Ghraib.

The Iraqis Take Power

As Iraqi capabilities grew, Iraqi officials became more assertive and less inclined to consult with US advisors. The Iraqi government wanted to speed up its assumption of full responsibility for Iraq. In February 2009, President Barack Obama announced that the last US combat troops would leave Iraq the following year; the last brigade withdrew on August 19, 2010. However, some 50,000 US troops remained in Iraq in an "advisory capacity" to help train Iraqi forces. Further, the United States announced that from 2011 it would also take charge of training the Iraqi police force.

Abu Ghraib

Abu Ghraib was a notorious prison near Baghdad where Saddam Hussein's secret police detained his enemies. After the invasion of Iraq, the prison was taken over by the U.S. military. In 2004, stories emerged of the ill-treatment of Iraqi detainees in the prison, and photographs showed US personnel humiliating and taunting prisoners. The harsh treatment of the prisoners caused concern in the United States and great resentment in the Muslim world.

May

June 30 Britain Islamists launch an unsuccessful attack on Glasgow airport.

April 18 Iraq Some 130 people die in a suicide attack on Sadriya market in Baghdad, the largest single attack for years.

May 12 Afghanistan The senior Taliban commander, Mullah Dadullah, is killed fighting US forces.

The Middle East

From 2001, the United States launched major initiatives across the region to remake the Middle East as part of its efforts to stop Islamic extremism from taking hold.

A Lebanese woman shows her support for Hezbollah, a Shiite group blamed for terror attacks in Israel. →→

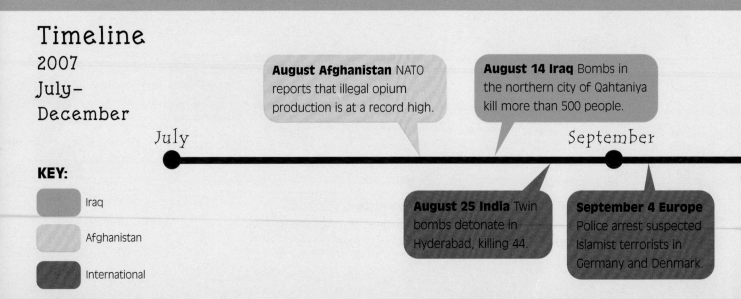

Timeline

2007
July–December

August Afghanistan NATO reports that illegal opium production is at a record high.

August 14 Iraq Bombs in the northern city of Qahtaniya kill more than 500 people.

July   September

August 25 India Twin bombs detonate in Hyderabad, killing 44.

September 4 Europe Police arrest suspected Islamist terrorists in Germany and Denmark.

KEY:

Iraq

Afghanistan

International

↑ A wanted poster shows suspected al-Qaeda members from Saudi Arabia and Yemen.

The United States aimed to transform a region that had sunk into economic stagnation, religious turmoil, and conflict. Al-Qaeda and other Islamist groups continued to draw support across the region. In part, their popularity reflects continuing resentment of the creation of Israel in 1948 on Arab-occupied land and of the Israeli treatment of their Palestinian neighbors.

Saudi Arabia

Saudi Arabia is one of the major regional powers and home to the most important Muslim holy sites. Saudi Arabia has two opposing political groups: modernists on one hand and

Timeline

June 24, 2002 President George W. Bush outlines a "road map" for peace that calls for an independent Palestinian state coexisting with Israel.

May 12, 2003 At least 35 people are killed in suicide attacks on Western compounds in the Saudi city of Riyadh.

December 12, 2003 President Bush signs the Syrian Accountability Act, which imposes trade and financial sanctions as punishment for Syria's support of terrorism.

December 6, 2004 Militants storm the US Consulate in Jeddah, Saudia Arabia, killing seven people.

August 15, 2005 Israel begins to pull out of the Gaza Strip.

November 9, 2005 Coordinated bomb attacks on hotels in Amman, Jordan, kill at least 60 people.

(continued page 36)

October 18 Pakistan Hours after her return to the country from exile, former president Benazir Bhutto survives bomb attacks that kill 136 of her followers.

December 16 Iraq UK forces hand control of the southern city of Basra to Iraqi forces.

November

November Pakistan The Pakistan military intensifies actions against Islamic militants in the Swat Valley.

December 27 Pakistan Benazir Bhutto is shot dead by an assassin who then blows himself up.

Timeline (continued)

January 26, 2006 The Islamist Hamas party wins Palestinian elections in Gaza.

June 28–November 26, 2006 The Second Intifada, or uprising, sees fighting between Israel and Palestine in the Gaza Strip.

July 12–August 14, 2006 War in Lebanon sees the Israelis claim victory over the Islamist Hezbollah movement.

May 20–September 7, 2007 A battle between the Islamist Fatah al-Islam party and the Lebanese army ends in victory for the army.

December 27, 2008–January 18, 2009 Israel attacks the Gaza Strip, and Hamas suffers heavy losses.

August 28, 2009 A suicide bomber blows himself up at a party in Jeddah attended by Prince Mohammed bin Nayef, head of Saudi security.

traditionalist Wahhabi clerics on the other. With half of all Saudis under the age of 20, and demanding economic development, the conservative clerics, who own many state institutions such as schools, face a considerable challenge.

The Road Map

The Arab-Israeli issue continues to dominate the region. A US-led "road map" that would lead to lasting peace failed. Despite an Israeli withdrawal from the Gaza Strip in late 2003, the Israelis continued to build settlements on occupied land in the West Bank. Meanwhile, Palestinian terrorists continued to kill dozens of Israeli citizens, often in suicide attacks.

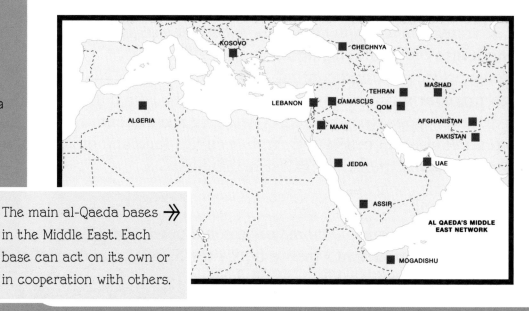

The main al-Qaeda bases → in the Middle East. Each base can act on its own or in cooperation with others.

Timeline
2008
January–June

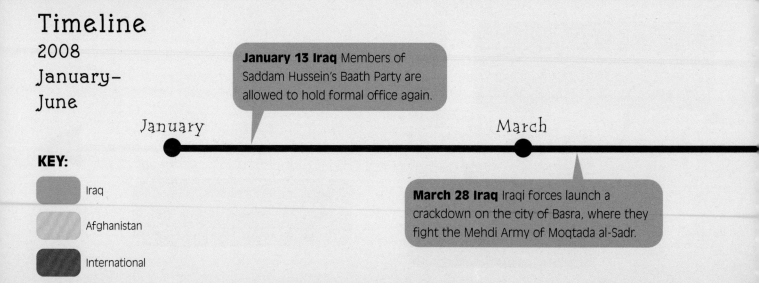

January

March

January 13 Iraq Members of Saddam Hussein's Baath Party are allowed to hold formal office again.

March 28 Iraq Iraqi forces launch a crackdown on the city of Basra, where they fight the Mehdi Army of Moqtada al-Sadr.

KEY:

Iraq

Afghanistan

International

← In 2006, Israel blockaded Lebanon to prevent supplies reaching Hezbollah.

The "War on Terror"

After the terrorist attacks of 9/11, 2001, Arab countries led by Syria, Egypt, and Jordan condemned the attacks and offered the United States assistance. However, in September 2002, when President Bush sought UN consent to invade Iraq as part of the "war on terror," all three countries voted against the invasion. Once the Iraq war began, they suffered economically, as they depended on Iraq for oil and trade.

Arab leaders were torn between reform and stability. Jordan introduced a form of parliamentary government. Syria, however, largely ignored its commitments to the United States' effort and continued to support terrorist groups.

Hamas

Hamas was founded in 1987 as an Islamist group that aimed to drive Israel from what it saw as Palestinian land. There was a tradition of terror attacks in the region, and Hamas's military brigade was notorious for carrying out suicide bombing raids within Israel. In 2006, Hamas won a majority in Palestinian elections and effectively took charge of Gaza.

← An Israeli soldier fires tear gas at Palestinian protestors in the West Bank.

May

June 14 Afghanistan In a jailbreak in Kandahar, more than 350 Taliban prisoners escape.

May 18 India The city of Jaipur is rocked by eight simultaneous bombs that kill 63 people.

June 17 Iraq A Shiite market is bombed in Baghdad, killing some 63 people.

Southeast Asia

Many terrorist groups that operate across Southeast Asia are not well known. Despite having different goals, many of them cooperate freely with each other.

An Indonesian wears a ➔ shirt bearing an image of Osama bin Laden. Some Indonesian Muslims see bin Laden as an Islamic hero.

Timeline
2008
July–
December

July 7 Afghanistan Pakistan is blamed for a suicide attack on the Indian Embassy in Kabul that kills 50 people.

September 20 Pakistan A car bomb at the popular Marriott hotel in Islamabad kills more than 60 and leaves 250 injured.

July

September

KEY:

◻ Iraq

◻ Afghanistan

◼ International

August Pakistan Another intense campaign against militants begins in the Swat Valley.

September 9 United States President George W. Bush announces sending 4,500 more US troops to Afghanistan in what is called a "quiet surge."

Southeast Asia has numerous different kinds of terrorist organizations, many of which are motivated by a fundamentalist interpretation of Islam. These organizations are characterized by a high degree of cooperation. Even insurgent groups that do not share the same goals cooperate across national boundaries. That allows them jointly to develop logistics and training, and to establish safe havens. For example, Jemaah Islamiyah, which is based in Indonesia and traditionally has very strong ties with al-Qaeda, has operated in the Philippines. Abu Sayyaf, which means "bearer of the sword" in Arabic, is a militant group based in the southern Philippines that seeks to create a separate Islamic state for the country's Muslim minority. The US government condemns Abu Sayyaf as a terrorist group that is linked to Osama bin Laden's al-Qaeda network.

Police in Indonesia stand guard at the trial of an alleged terrorist. ⇒

Timeline

October 12, 2002 Bombs in nightclubs on Bali, Indonesia, kill 202 people. Jemaah Islamiyah is blamed; the United States lists it as a terrorist organization.

August 5, 2003 A car bomb at the Marriott Hotel in Jakarta, Indonesia, kills 12.

August 12, 2003 Riduan Isamuddin, known as Hambali, the suspected planner of the Bali bombings, is captured.

September 9, 2004 A bomb attack on the Australian Embassy in Jakarta.

October 1, 2005 Suicide bombers hit tourist area of Bali, killing 20 people and injuring more than 130.

August 12, 2007 In Jakarta, the Islamist Hizb ut-Tahrir group calls for the creation of a single caliphate across the Muslim world.

(continued page 40)

November 16 Iraq The Iraqi Parliament approves a security pact with the United States under which all US troops will leave Iraq by the end of 2011.

November

December

November 26–29 India Gunmen launch attacks on eight sites in Mumbai, including railroad stations and tourist hotels; there are 173 confirmed dead. The attackers are thought to be sponsored by Pakistan.

December Pakistan Press reports claim that Islamic militants now control 75 percent of the Swat Valley.

Timeline (continued)

November 9, 2008 Three members of Jemaah Islamiyah are executed for 2002 Bali bombings.

July 17, 2009 Two suicide bombs in Marriott and Ritz-Carlton hotels in Jakarta kill nine.

September 17, 2009 Indonesian police shoot dead the country's most-wanted Islamist militant, Noordin Mohammad Top.

September 21, 2009 The Philippine army captures a commander of the Moro Islamic Liberation Front.

March 10, 2010 The mastermind of the Bali bombings, Dulmatin, is confirmed dead.

A US airman shows his Filipino counterparts how to use emergency equipment. ⇒

Intelligence Failures

Recent developments in the war on terrorism have made Southeast Asia central to the US strategy to defeat terrorism. However, many of Southeast Asia's terrorist groups are not on the US State Department's list of Foreign Terrorist Organizations (FTO). This means that current policies attack only a portion of the broader terrorist network.

⤊ A leader of the Moro Islamic Liberation Front is arrested in the Philippines.

In addition, although terrorists in Southeast Asia work closely together, their governments often do not. The terrorists take advantage of this poor regional cooperation to hide from the authorities by moving to the country next door.

Government Weakness

Terrorist groups have sought refuge in areas where local authorities are least

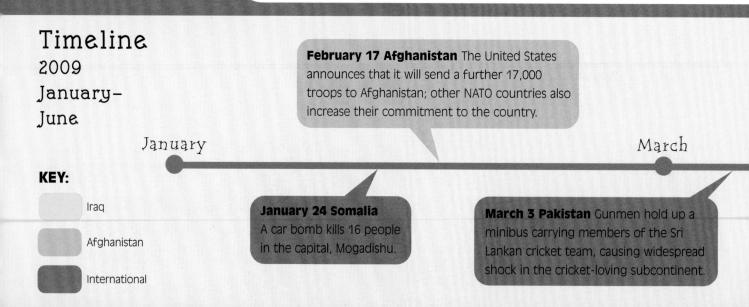

Timeline
2009
January–June

January

February 17 Afghanistan The United States announces that it will send a further 17,000 troops to Afghanistan; other NATO countries also increase their commitment to the country.

March

KEY:

Iraq

Afghanistan

International

January 24 Somalia A car bomb kills 16 people in the capital, Mogadishu.

March 3 Pakistan Gunmen hold up a minibus carrying members of the Sri Lankan cricket team, causing widespread shock in the cricket-loving subcontinent.

committed to countering terrorism, most notably in Indonesia and the Philippines.

The Filipino government may be the weakest link in Southeast Asia's antiterrorist efforts. There have been few terrorist arrests in the Philippines. The existence of a safe haven in Mindanao in the southern Philippines permits Southeast Asia's terrorist brotherhood to plan and train. However, in 2009 and 2010, government forces again achieved some minor but promising victories against both Abu Sayyaf and Jemaah Islamiyah. The same period saw the Indonesian government also make some breakthroughs.

Indonesian police walk past wreckage after the ↓ Bali bombing of 2002.

The Bali Bombs

On October 12, 2002, three explosions rocked the resort of Kuta on the island of Bali in Indonesia. The main targets were popular nightclubs. A total of 202 people died, with 240 injured; of the dead, 38 were Indonesians and 88 were Australian tourists. The attacks were the most deadly episode in the struggle by extremists to establish an Islamic state in Southeast Asia. The group Jemaah Islamiyah was blamed. Three of its members were executed for the crime in 2008.

March 27 United States President Barack Obama announces a new strategy including sending a further 4,000 personnel to Afghanistan.

June 10 Afghanistan General Stanley McChrystal takes over as commander of US forces as part of an attempt to break the deadlock.

June

June 30 Iraq Iraqis celebrate their "day of sovereignty" as US troops withdraw from Iraq towns and cities.

The United States

While the US public grew increasingly skeptical about the wars in Iraq and Afghanistan, the fear of homegrown terrorist attacks continued.

A watchtower guards the fence at the prison camp at Guantanamo Bay in Cuba. →

Timeline
2009 July– December

July 2 Afghanistan US troops launch a massive offensive against the Taliban in southern Helmand province.

September 17 Somalia Terrorists bomb the African Union base at Mogadishu.

July

September

August United States President Obama announces that all US troops will leave Iraq by August 2010.

KEY:

Iraq

Afghanistan

International

↑ Two F-16s fly over San Francisco in a training exercise to deal with a terrorist attack.

In December 2001, 92 percent of Americans told pollsters that they were satisfied with US progress in the "war on terror." Ten years later, in January 2011, after the invasion of and withdrawal from Iraq, that figure had fallen to 39 percent.

Negative Perceptions

The decline in the war's popularity had many causes, including a series of scandals. In 2004, photographs emerged of US personnel mistreating Iraqi detainees in the prison at Abu Ghraib. The Central Intelligence Agency was accused of torturing suspected terrorists.

Timeline

October 7, 2001 President Bush announces Operation Enduring Freedom, which will send troops to Afghanistan to fight the Taliban.

October 26, 2001 President Bush signs the Patriot Act, which gives authorities wide powers to fight terrorism.

December 22, 2001 Richard Reid, a British national, tries to detonate a bomb hidden in his shoe on a Miami-bound flight.

January 11, 2002 Prisoners arrive at Guantanamo Bay, Cuba.

November 25, 2002 President Bush signs the Homeland Security Act into law.

March 20, 2003 US troops lead the invasion of Iraq.

April 28, 2004 The popular CBS *60 Minutes* show reports on alleged abuse at the Abu Ghraib prison in Baghdad by US military personnel.

(continued page 44)

November 5 United States A Muslim US Army major, Nidal Malik Hasan, shoots dead 13 people at Fort Hood in Texas; 30 people are wounded.

December 1 United States Barack Obama announces a further 30,000 US troops will be sent to Afghanistan, raising the total to 100,000.

November

November 2 Afghanistan Hamid Kharzai's reelection as president is confirmed.

December Iraq A group linked to al-Qaeda is blamed for a wave of suicide bombs in Baghdad.

December 25 United States A Nigerian attempts to blow up an airliner flying from Paris to Detroit; his bomb only sets fire to his underwear.

Timeline (continued)

January 20, 2009 Barack Obama is sworn in as the 44th president of the United States.

January 22, 2009 President Obama orders the closure of Guantanamo Bay.

November 5, 2009 US Army major Nidal Malik Hasan, a Muslim, shoots dead 13 people at Fort Hood, Texas.

December 25, 2009 A Nigerian attempts to blow up a Detroit-bound flight.

May 1, 2010 A car bomb is diffused in Times Square, New York, with no casualties.

August 19, 2010 The last US troops leave Iraq.

May 1, 2011 US special forces kill Osama bin Laden during a raid in Abbottabad, Pakistan.

An expert examines the car bomb found in Times Square in 2010. ⟶

Many Americans were troubled by the detention of prisoners at a US base in Guantanamo Bay, Cuba. The prisoners were classed as "enemy combatants" and held in harsh conditions, without trial. After Barack Obama became president in January 2009, he announced plans to transfer prisoners to the mainland.

Falling Optimism

The decline in the war's popularity also reflected growing US casualties. Some 4,301 American service personnel died in Iraq, and more than 31,000 had been injured; in Afghanistan, as troop numbers increased in 2009, some 714 had been killed.

As the cost of the war rose, optimism fell. In May 2003, George W. Bush announced that the military

Timeline
2010
January–December

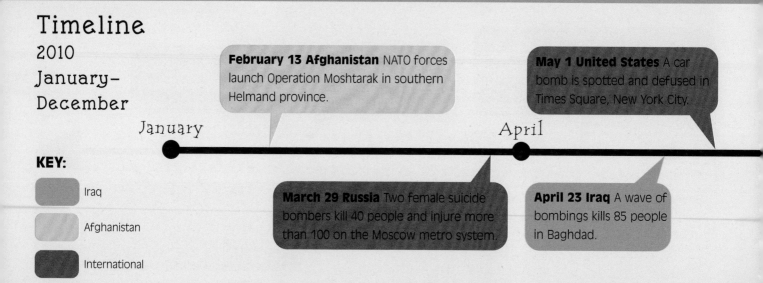

KEY:

- Iraq
- Afghanistan
- International

January

April

February 13 Afghanistan NATO forces launch Operation Moshtarak in southern Helmand province.

May 1 United States A car bomb is spotted and defused in Times Square, New York City.

March 29 Russia Two female suicide bombers kill 40 people and injure more than 100 on the Moscow metro system.

April 23 Iraq A wave of bombings kills 85 people in Baghdad.

← US demonstrators protest against the PATRIOT Act of 2001.

struggle in Iraq had been won. Despite more than 160,000 US troops in the country, however, terrorists continued to strike. Iraqi civilians died in high numbers, while the government was unable to establish strong governance. In Afghanistan, too, the Taliban proved a difficult enemy. Even after the US withdrawal from Iraq in 2010, some Americans worried that the "war on terror" could not be won.

Homegrown Plots

At home, while the PATRIOT Act of 2001 remained controversial, plots by American Islamists failed or were thwarted. They included an attempt to detonate a car bomb in Times Square, New York City, in May 2010; the bomb was defused after it was spotted by police.

The PATRIOT Act

Passed in October 2001, the USA PATRIOT Act aimed to improve the ability of security services to prevent terrorism. The act improved communications between agencies, for example. It also increased official powers to monitor both immigrants and citizens, including by reading their mail or listening to phone calls. Many people protested that such powers were a breach of civil liberties.

← Lines at airports are a visible sign of increased security.

July 20 Afghanistan An international conference endorses President Karzai's plan for the future security of the country.

September 29 Europe Police thwart planned gun and bomb attacks in France, Britain, and Germany.

July

December

August 19 Iraq The last US combat brigade leaves Iraq seven years after the invasion.

December 11 Sweden Two car bombs in the center of Stockholm kill an Islamist bomber and injure two people.

Glossary

alliance An agreement between countries to cooperate.

arms embargo A ban on selling or transporting arms to a particular government or country.

caliphate A spiritual Islamic government ruled by a caliph; some Muslims want to establish a caliphate that stretches across many countries.

coalition The temporary uniting of different forces, such as countries or political parties.

drone An unmanned aircraft that is guided by remote control.

extremism A belief in an extreme version of views or opinions.

fundamentalist Someone who believes in a very simple, black-and-white form of a religion.

governance The act of governing a country.

hijack To seize an airplane or other means of transportation and force it to go to a particular destination.

intelligence Information about the intentions or operations of an enemy.

intifada A Palestinian uprising against the Israeli government.

Islamist A Muslim who believes that society should be organized according to the laws of Islam.

militia An unofficial citizen army.

Muslim A follower of Islam.

nationalist Someone who believes that his or her nation and its interests are more important than all others.

radical Someone who holds extreme political or religious views.

safe haven A place where an individual or group is protected by the government.

separatists People who want to separate a particular region from a country, either to become independent or to become part of another country.

Shiite A Muslim who follows a minority version of Islam that is particularly strong in Iran.

suicide bomber Someone who carries out a bombing attack during which he or she will also be killed by the bomb.

Sunni A Muslim who follows the majority version of Islam.

terrorist Someone who tries to achieve political goals by using random acts of violence to cause widespread fear.

Further Reading

Books

Adams, Simon. *The Iraq War* (Secret History). Arcturus Publishing, 2011.

Barr, Gary. *War on Terror: Is the World a Safer Place?* (Behind the News). Heinemann-Raintree, 2008.

Crawford, Steve. *War on Terror* (Facts at Your Fingertips). Brown Bear Books, 2010.

Downing, David. *The War on Terror* (Timelines). Arcturus Publishing, 2007.

Ellis, Deborah. *Off to War: Voices of Soldiers' Children.* Groundwood Books, 2008.

Gerber, Larry. *The Taliban in Afghanistan.* Rosen Classroom, 2010.

Gupta, Dipak K. *Who Are the Terrorists?* (The Roots of Terrorism). Chelsea House Publications, 2006.

Miller, Mara. *Remembering September 11, 2001: What We Know Now.* Enslow Publishers, 2011.

Rushmann, Paul. *The War on Terror* (Point/Counterpoint). Chelsea House Publications, 2008.

Tracy, Kathleen. *The Story of September 11, 2001* (Monumental Milestones). Mitchell Lane Publishers, 2009.

Williams, Brian. *The War on Terror* (Secret History). Arcturus Publishing, 2011.

Websites

http://news.bbc.co.uk/1/hi/in_depth/ world/2001/war_on_terror
BBC news site special report on Investigating al-Qaeda.

http://www.globalissues.org/issue/245 /war-on-terror
Edition of Global Issues that focuses on the war on terror.

http://www.september11news.com/
An in-depth archive of world reaction to the terrorist attacks of 9/11, 2001.

http://www.globalsecurity.org/ military/ops/enduring-freedom.htm
Global Security page with links to historical and ongoing aspects of Operation Enduring Freedom.

http://www.history.army.mil/
Home page of the US Army Center of Military History, with links to online features and exhibitions.

Index

Abu Ghraib 33, 43
Abu Sayyaf 39, 41
Afghanistan 4, 8, 9, 10, 11, 13, 14, 15, 16, 17, 27, 29, 42, 44, 45
Africa 18, 19, 20, 24, 25
Arab 8, 35, 37
Arab-Israeli issue 36
Atta, Mohamed 8
axis of evil 11
Baghdad 30
Bali bombing 41
Battle of Tora Bora 13, 17
Beslan school siege 23, 24
Bhutto, Benazir 29
bin Laden, Osama 8, 9, 10, 11, 12, 13, 15, 17, 27, 39
Bush, George W. 4, 11, 12, 31, 32, 37, 44
Chechnya 24
coalition 4, 12, 13, 14
de Menezes, Jean Charles 25
Egypt 8, 37
Ethiopia 20, 21
Europe 4, 15, 16, 22, 23, 24
extremism 13, 34, 41
Flight 93 9
Foreign Terrorist Organizations 40
fundamentalist 4, 12, 15, 39
Gaza Strip 36, 37
Ground Zero 11
Guantanamo Bay 42, 44
Hamas 37
Hezbollah 34, 37
hijackers 7, 8, 9
Horn of Africa 5, 13, 18, 20
Hussein, Saddam 4, 30, 31, 33
India 26, 28, 29
Indonesia 9, 39, 41
International Security Assistance Force (ISAF) 14, 16
Iraq 4, 8, 11, 20, 25, 30, 31, 32, 33, 37, 42, 43, 44, 45
Islamist 4, 6, 19, 21, 22, 24, 35, 37, 45
Israel 34, 35, 36, 37
Jordan 37
Kabul 10, 15, 16, 17
Koran 4
Lebanon 34, 37
London bombings 22, 25
Madrid bombings 24, 25
Middle East 34, 36
militants 28, 39
Mohammed, Khalid Sheikh 8
Moro Islamic Liberation Front 40
Moscow attacks 24
Multinational Force–Iraq 32
Mumbai attacks 26, 28, 29
Muslim 4, 8, 12, 13, 15, 19, 21, 24, 25, 32, 33, 35, 39
New People's Army (NPA) 38
9/11 attacks 7, 8, 11, 12, 15, 37
North Atlantic Treaty Organization (NATO) 12, 14, 15, 16, 17, 29
Northern Alliance 10, 13, 15
Obama, Barack 33, 44
Operation Enduring Freedom 5, 13
Operation Iraqi Freedom (OIF) 31
Pakistan 13, 15, 17, 26, 27, 28, 29
Palestine 35, 36, 37
PATRIOT Act 9, 45
Pentagon 7, 19
Petraeus, David 32
Philippines 13, 38, 39, 40, 41
Provincial Reconstruction Teams (PRTs) 16, 17
radical 9, 12, 20, 21
Russia 23, 24
Saudi Arabia 8, 29, 35
Shabab, al- 21
Shiite 32, 34
Somalia 19, 20, 21
Southeast Asia 38, 39, 40, 41
Sudan 20, 21
suicide bombing 8, 22, 24, 25, 37
Sunni 32
Syria 37
Taliban 4, 9, 10, 11, 12, 13, 15, 17, 27, 28, 45
United Nations (UN) 12, 21
Washington, DC 7, 8
weapons of mass destruction 16, 31
World Trade Center 6, 7, 11